© Elena Favela

## *About the Author*

KRISTIN NACA received her Ph.D. in English from University of Nebraska in 2008, an M.F.A. in poetry from University of Pittsburgh in 2003, and an M.A. in English linguistics from University of Cincinnati in 2000. Her poems have appeared in *The Cincinnati Review*, *Crab Orchard Review*, *Octopus Magazine*, and *Prairie Schooner*. She has been a member of the Macondo Workshop in San Antonio, Texas, since 2002. She teaches at Macalester College in St. Paul, Minnesota.

# BIRD
# EATING
# BIRD

The National Poetry Series was established in 1978 to ensure the publication of five poetry books annually through five participating publishers. Publication is funded by the Lannan Foundation; Stephen Graham; Joyce & Seward Johnson Foundation; Glenn and Renee Schaeffer, Juliet Lea Hillman Simonds Foundation; and Charles B. Wright III.

## 2008 Open Competition Winners

Anna Journey of Houston, Texas, *If Birds Gather Your Hair for Nesting*
Chosen by Thomas Lux, to be published by University of Georgia Press

Douglas Kearney of Van Nuys, California, *The Black Automaton*
Chosen by Catherine Wagner, to be published by Fence Books

Adrian Matejka of Edwardsville, Illinois, *Mixology*
Chosen by Kevin Young, to be published by Penguin Books

Kristin Naca of Minneapolis, Minnesota, *Bird Eating Bird*
Chosen by Yusef Komunyakaa for the National Poetry Series MTVU
    Prize, to be published by Harper Perennial

Sarah O'Brien of Brookfield, Ohio, *catch light*
Chosen by David Shapiro, to be published by Coffee House Press

# BIRD
# EATING
# BIRD

· POEMS ·

## KRISTIN NACA

HARPER ◉ PERENNIAL

NEW YORK · LONDON · TORONTO · SYDNEY · NEW DELHI · AUCKLAND

NATIONAL
ENDOWMENT
FOR THE ARTS
A great nation
deserves great art.

HARPER ● PERENNIAL

HarperCollins books may be purchased for educational, business, or sales promotional use. For information please write: Special Markets Department, HarperCollins Publishers, 10 East 53rd Street, New York, NY 10022.

FIRST EDITION

*Illustration of bird and book design by Justin Dodd*

Library of Congress Cataloging-in-Publication Data is available upon request.

ISBN 978-0-06-178234-3

09  10  11  12  13    ID/RRD    10  9  8  7  6  5  4  3  2  1

*In memory of beloved teacher and mentor, Carl Mills*

# CONTENTS

# ACKNOWLEDGMENTS

The generosity of so many enabled me to complete this collection. I owe the greatest debt to my family: Christian and Lisa, Michael, Rosalin, Puring, Ralph and Mary. And my family: Julianne McAdoo, Nikki Ono, Bill and Alejandro Sanchez, Roger Solis, Arturo Madrid and Antonia Castañeda, Omar Rodríguez and Verónica Prida, my Elena, Jim Clawson, Vicente Lozano, Carla Trujillo and Leslie Larson, Anel Flores, Chris Cuomo and Karen Schlanger, Erin Flanagan, Maxine Leckie, Derek Walker, Chris Byrne, Leah and Macauley Devun, Stacey Berry and Andre Jordan, Barbara Banfield, Kate Nelson, Padrino, Madrina, and the Macondistas.

Thanks to many professors and writing teachers who responded to my work with generosity. Special thanks goes to my committee members at University of Pittsburgh and University of Nebraska. For their wisdom and unflinching belief, thank you, Sandra Cisneros and Hilda Raz.

To my friends who wore down their fingernails against my drafts: Dina Rhoden, Nancy Krygowski, Heather Green, Mathias Svalina, Jehanne Dubrow, Lois Williams, Jan Beatty, Ellen Placey Wadey, Jeff Oaks, Chingbee Cruz, Renato Rosaldo, Diana Delgado, Marcia Ochoa, Nick Carbó, Eileen Tabios, Hadara Bar-Nadav, and Chuck Rybak. For all their timely advice: John Marshall and Christine Deavel of Open Books. Thank you, Joy, for your horses.

Special thanks to María L. Lorenzo, at University of Nebraska, whose generous feedback and encouragement made my writing poems in Spanish possible. Thanks to Hedgebrook, and UN-L, for providing fellowships and time to write. Thanks to my colleagues at Macalester College. Thanks to painter Heather Hagle for her friendship and vision. And thanks to the National Poetry Series for the support of my work, Michael Signorelli at Harper Perennial for his enthusiasm, Yusef Komunyakaa, and everyone at MTV for giving me "My Shot with Yusef Komunyakaa."

These poems originally appeared in the following venues:

*5AM*: "While Watching *Dallas*, My Auntie Grooms Me for Work at the Massage Parlor"

*THE ASIAN PACIFIC AMERICAN JOURNAL*: "Grocery Shopping with my Girlfriend Who Is Not Asian"

*THE CINCINNATI REVIEW*: "Heart Like a Clock"

*CRAB ORCHARD REVIEW*: "Uses for Spanish in Pittsburgh"

*HARPUR PALATE*: "Baptism," "In the Time of the Caterpillars"

*INDIANA REVIEW*: "*Todavía no*," "Not Yet"

*THE NORTH AMERICAN REVIEW*: "What I Don't Tell My Children about the Philippines"

*OCHO: THE MiPOesias PRINT JOURNAL COMPANION*: "Speaking English Is Like," "Glove," "Adoration at El Montan"

*PINOY POETICS: A COLLECTION OF AUTOBIOGRAPHICAL AND CRITICAL ESSAYS ON FILIPINO AND FILIPINO AMERICAN POETICS*: "Language Poetry / Grandma's English"

*OCTOPUS*: "House"

*PRAIRIE SCHOONER*: "Ode to Glass," "One Foot," "*Las Meninas* / The Maids of Honor," "Rear Window," "Witness"

*RIO GRANDE REVIEW*: "Speaking Spanish Goes Like This"

*RIO GRANDE REVIEW ONLINE*: "Catching Cardinals"

Her Spanish sounds like sunlight drying a wet shirt.
And in the process, I've grown fond of her.

She's *delicadeza*, a word that names her nature.
Whose dream deepens in the rain? Whose hair is lilacs?

—*Eugene Gloria*

# SPEAKING ENGLISH IS LIKE

Brown and beige and blonde tiles set in panels of tile across the
bathroom floor.

Wakes curled into the pavement by traffic, the asphalt a slow, gray tide.

A loose floorboard hiding the gouges chunked out of the floor.

Tawny red curtains hamstrung in the quick, morning light.

Her body oils like sage in a shirt, in the bed sheets.

Pigeons on a line and in the gutters.

The staple that misfires and jams the hammer.

The tender, black wick at the top of a candle's waxy lip.

The lonely woman secretly dying her curtains red at the Laundry
Factory.

The purple and purple-blue berry sacks tethered to a blackberry rind.

Branches lolled by the weight of voluminous, tender sacks.

The path along the lake lit up with the pitch of purple stars.

Mouthfuls of lavender at the height of August.

Her lips, red gathering in the creases when she puckers.

Endings that are dirty tricks and also feathers.

Red water out the pipes, teeming from the rusty gutters.

The curtain flicker in the leafy, August breeze.

The ghostly cu-cu echoing through the purple night, under stars.

## TODAVÍA NO

Los pedazos de la lengua quedan tan gordos y abultados como flores.

Dime, árbol. Son los que están allá solamente ramas desnudas y alguna
corteza.

Todavía no, no hay palabras para hacer capas de piel sobre la primavera.

El color verde se difumina sin *leaves*.

El único pájaro que aterriza allí es el halcón.

En el espejo, el reflejo de su pelo es castañas labradas.

Las venas de la cala están labradas con paredes. No, piedras. No,
pérdidas.

Mientras tanto, tus manos están hechas de nudillos y hechas de piel.

En la ventana, el cristal se superpone al árbol desnudo afuera.

Sin *fingernails*, solamente clavos. *Los dedos-garras. Los dedos-lanzas*,
dice ella.

La ropa en la cama está limpia y suelta.

La mujer en la cama espera no morir mientras duerme... *despierta...*
*despierta*.

El halcón la aguada en el árbol desnudo, más allá de la ventana, más allá
de los muros.

La canción del pájaro superpone a la noche despejada, la deja despierta.

Todavía no, todas las canciones que canta, le da de comer al halcón.

Todas las noches que espera ella, le da de comer a la muerte.

# NOT YET

The nubs of the tongue sit fat and bulky as flowers.

Say, *tree*. What's there but bare branches and some bark.

No words for putting layers of skin on spring yet.

Green glows loose without its leaves.

The only bird that lands there is the falcon.

In the mirror, the reflection of her hair is carved chestnuts.

The veins of the creek encrusted with walls. No, stones. No, losing.

Meanwhile your hands are made of knuckles and made of skin.

In the window, glass overlaps the naked tree outside.

No fingernails, just the nails. *Finger-claws. Finger-swords*, she says.

The laundry on the bed is clean and limp.

The woman in her bed hopes she doesn't die in her sleep . . . *wake up* . . .
   *wake up*.

The falcon waits for her in the naked tree, beyond the window, beyond
   the walls.

The small bird's song overlaps the clear night, keeps her from her sleep.

Still, every song he sings, he's food for the falcon.

Every night she waits, she's food for death.

## "GAVILÁN O PALOMA"

*—Mexico City*

Once a bird pecked her lover's hand
with such sincerity that she lost
hold of the seeds she secretly tossed,
to keep all the birds at her command.

»«

*No dejabas de mirar,* you sang me,           *you didn't stop staring*
last night, *estabas sola completamente*     *you alone were completely*
*bella y sensual,* and the notes stirred          *beautiful and sensual*
loose feather dust from your chest.

When you exhaled, your silhouette
dissolved, reddening the D. F. dusk.
Vibrato frayed your veil: how you fled
one city, but betrayal beckoned you;

confess, how lovers nest in branches
of your collarbones while you sleep.
*Entre tus brazos caí* . . . consumed            *How I fell into your arms*
by your song's, lonesome downbeat.

»«

6

*Paloma,*

I know some days begin with birds.

Nights we suffer from too few songs.

How the chorus of a woman's lips delays

Sorrows that each heartbeat prolongs.

Amiga,

Tell me how you're leaning, before

sunlight bathes the city in pink spells.

Will your voice deliver me morning?

Or, will the caroling street-vendors bells?

# USES FOR SPANISH IN PITTSBURGH

What use is there for describing
Bloomfield's hard-sloping rooftops this way?
Or that the church steeples beam upward, inexpertly
toward God. What difference does it make
to say, the chimney pipes peel their red skins,
or *las pieles rojas*, exposing tough steel underneath.

What good, then, for Spanish,
its parity of consonants and vowels—
vowels like a window to the throat,
breath chiming through the vocal chords.
And what good is singing to describe
this barrio's version of the shortened sky,
*el cielo cortado*—power lines crisscrossing
so high, that blue only teases through them.

And what for fog *la niebla arrastra*,
creeping down *las calles inmóviles*
before the bank and grocery store open.
*Y por la zapatería* on Liberty Avenue,                *And by the shoemaker's*
a lady's antique boot for a street sign.

What use to remember in any language
my father was a Puerto Rican shoe salesman.
From his mouth dangled a ropy, ashy cigarette.
He spoke good English and knew when to smile.

With his strong fingers he'd knot shoes like *redes*,                    *fishing nets*
knew three kinds of knots so lady customers
could buy the shoes they loved to look at
but really shouldn't have worn.

At home, Dad kept his *lengua íntima*
to himself. His Spanish not for children,
only older relatives who forced him to speak,
reminded, *Spanish means there's another person
inside you*. All beauty, he'd argue, no power in it.
Still, I remember, he spoke a hushed Spanish
to customers who struggled in English, the ones
he pitied for having no language to live on.

So many years gone, what use to invent
or question him in Pittsburgh? The educated one,
why would I want my clumsy Spanish to stray
from the pages of books outward? My tongue,
he'd think so untrue and inarticulate. Each word
having no past in it. What then? Speaking Spanish
to make them better times or Pittsburgh
a better place. *En vez de regresar la dura realidad*        *Instead of returning*
*del pasado*. And then, if I choose to speak like this        *to the hard reality*
who will listen?                                                                      *of the past*

## ODE TO GLASS

After its lip
the bottle flares out
like the A-line of
a girl's skirt
when she twirls
at recess.

On the descent
the company's crest—
one red and one blue
crescent about to
clasp together
into a globe
but between
them, the name
of the soda sits
in bold, white letters.

Below
the slogan
the tiny print:
*contenido neto 355 ml,*
and *hecho en México,*
in perfectly
executed paint.

Partway down
the bottle corners
into a barrel-shape,
the swiveled glass,
the same as stripes
of a barber's pole, forces
the eye to follow
and twist along its
blurred contours,
the way skin blurs
the contours of
an arm so you
slow down into
the elbow's nook.

And how much
like skin the peach
and brown and blue
reflections inside
the glass lend it
dimension while outside
the surface and shape
are seamless, but
for some stitching
underneath, a zipper
dialed around the
bottle's base to
serve as feet.

And where
the glass corners
from cone to barrel
a ring carved from
the bottles being
packed too close
and rubbing together
in their crates.

Scars that
keep dry and
soft as silk, even as
the glass beads, and
you start to trace
the droplets back
over the powder,
and still dry after
you've swabbed up
the condensation
and your fingers
have gone clumsy
from the bottle's
brittle sweat.

When the bottle's
this cold, the swivels
of glass are charged,
icy bulbs that steal
heat from the nubs
of your fingertips,

so you rub them
to your forehead
and feel nothing
but your own heat
swirl back and forth
from your head
to your hand.

Each time you drink—
the bubbles rising up
through the sweet,
brown liquid, stirring
your nose, then lips—
how easily details
of time slip away and
you're seven-years-old
again drinking Pepsi
at the *sari-sari* store
next to Uncle Ulpe's
house in Manila. And
you guzzle it down.

# BAPTISM

The taller men with baseball bats, a tree branch garbled with knots,
log iron, and leftover pipe from the fence they put up last summer.
The shorter men gripping buck knives for slashing at the pig's neck.
And ripened on a dry slop of peanuts, cornflakes, and newspaper
shavings, moiled between the washer and dryer and shelves of dust-caked
soda bottles, the pig that grew tall enough to sniff and lick the doorknob.
So, from the other side, I watched it turn and, hearing it flicker at night,
dreamt of succoring the pig's escape. Then, they unleashed it. It
drumming its blunt, fleshy hammers through the downstairs hallway,
its high-pitched cough the air it dragged over vocal chord lathing.
Then, they prodded it across the yard and cornered it under the porch.
So with a *ka-thunk* the pig, then stilled in its tracks, had to watch
as one of the men crept up and dragged a knife across its neck.
They held the sullen body in their pink, craggy hands, standing up,
in order to catch its blood in a bucket. Blood Mother cooked
into a musty, black blood-food we smothered our rice in. After that,
the men heaved the body on a picnic table wrapped in Glad bags
and tape and rolled the carcass on its back and split the skin down
the long belly, its guts oozing out—all beigy, peachy, and blue like
clouds of chewed bubble-gum or the bulbs of a wilted, worn-in coin purse.
Collapsed hoses, too soft and slick to pile up, spread across the lawn
in pearly pools. Then, carefully, the men excised the gall bladder
before it broke and spoiled the meat, gallbladder curled like a finger
on a folding chair beside them while they emptied the carcass to the snout.
On the grass, the heart and lungs lay, and the throat ridged and perfect
as a staircase. And then, the new backbone a metal rod they pierced

and guided through the carcass. Tackle they hoisted onto some posts, so—though I can't remember exactly—they could turn the whole thing on a spit. How it hovered for hours over the orange coals that startled whenever the juices dripped, and the rangy smell of singed pork-meat and charcoal slinked into our sweat, and the pork skin transluted, cells shimmering amber and snapping easily to the touch, hot loosened fat down our fingers, until the meat fell apart without having to hack at it. The men, smoking packs of Kool cigarettes and piling up the empty Schlitz beer cans, hardly mentioning a thing about the child.

# ONE FOOT

Listen and you'll hear a knock.
Watch the dust lift off the land.
Pray I give up my cane and walk.

Some wind will tear the ears off stalks
Of corn; no sound eviscerates the strand.
I listen close, but hear no knock.

Each footstep, I mill bones to chalk.
Then, sink in soot wherever I stand.
I dream I give up my cane and walk.

In nightmares, wispy pipe-roots block
The blood flow to a leaf-foot, browning, orphaned
On the stem. Listless, I hear the knock

Of the oxygen machine. The good doc
Strings me up a foot, leaves me bland,
Yellow toes. "Go ahead and walk,"

Doc says and hacks the cast to a caulk
Of gauze, peat hair, and loose, tanned
Skin Nurse swabs. Like clockwork knock

Gulls at my windowsill. That bad flock,
The smallest sores pique their demands.
Listen. Do you hear them knock?
Do I pray harder? Wake up. Walk.

## GROCERY SHOPPING WITH MY GIRLFRIEND
## WHO IS NOT ASIAN

Through the doors gleam pyramids
of apples, peaches, broccoli hybrids.
I pronounce a name in Minh, *kài lán*,
pull back its leaves, and reveal small,
white flowers. All to watch her mouth
the words and make white flowers
translations. She asks what *uppo* is
and I tell her how my auntie grew
the woody fruit by foot-long beans,
tomatoes my father claimed to grow
on his own. If she needs more, I'll list
ingredients like a poem, like garlic
onion, ground pork, and potatoes.
Vegetables I don't have words for
stew for an hour in that poem.

We don't last long before the blitz
of shiny packaging overwhelms her.
One sea green cellophane submits
to a lime, pea, then a teal wrapper,
the lucky elephant or lotus stamp,
the photographs of curious
food items that luxuriate in broth,
a cartoon sketch of a boy's face
above some steam lines and a bowl—
delight the angle that his eyes slant

as he devours the noodles. Brands
we differentiate by script, each lilt
depicts the path a language takes
to conquer, infiltrate, or drift.
Some brushstrokes end in a tip
sharp as my tongue when I dish out
old-fashioned, Asian lady barking.

The aisles feed into a basin where
aquariums line the walls, and fish
glint beneath fluorescent light bulbs.
When I say, *So gorgeous, I feel guilty
eating them*, that's not the half of it.
Next week, we trade-in excess beauty
to shop at the markets my Mother
took me—and I still shop as though
my girlfriend and I had never met,
where we fish beans from boxes;
dodge old ladies throwing elbows
at the fruit bins; scales unraveling
off a fish when a butcher knocks
the daylights out of it. And in time
come the meals we dine on chicken
that stinks of piss-soaked feathers.

# LANGUAGE POETRY / GRANDMA'S ENGLISH

*Dos / doze / those / toes* shuffles through my head
when Grandma speaks, consonants blurred
from her mouth a flat tire. Unable to make out
each word I try reading lips, *What / that / cat woman*,
but end up lost. Her lips relaxed, bursts of sound
fretting through them. *You muddy her,* Grandma barks
at my father. *You muddy her, she drives you grazy.*

A child, I love their arguments, never fully
understanding what Grandma means when
she tells Dad, *She get you rosin / rousing / rosing.*
*You watch. She geep driving you grazy.* Though
I do get when Grandma says, */ gahng /,* for *can,*
and when she says, */ gahng /,* for *can't.*
When she curses, wants sympathy—like,
*/ Gahng / it raw meat. It gives you gancer.*
*Look it's / rrrud /,* she blusters. Her *r*
like she's starting a lawn mower. */ Rrraw / meat,*
*Charlie,* she argues, shows it to my father.

*Marinade,* he answers. And Grandma gives up.
A martyr she says, *Go on, it it.* Her tongue
forcing sparks from our household English.
Beauty when she grabs her chest and sighs,
*I gahng go up dos stairs, Charlie. My art, my art!*

O the Eyes that will see me,
And the Mouth that will kiss me.
And the Rose I will stand on,
And the Hand that will turn me.

—*José García Villa*

## TRES MUJERES

1.

She watches from the chair.
Two lovers unlock the hatches
of each other's shirts. Crowbarring
of their wasp-sprung mouths where lips
eave together. Their bras barbed
to the bed. When their arms sigh
into place       the fireplace toolery.

In an hour or so the phone rings.
The receiver from her paw—knuckles
fast and cum-crusted—to the spotty
drop cloth. In her ear the rumpus
it's 10:00       it's 10:00

2.\*

across the bed       *h  h  h*

*h*  all the air at her back

*h*  breath on her neck and neck on her lips

*h*  quickened over a scissor leg

when  *h*  threads her arm across the other lovers

                                        she scores homophones

*there     ~~their~~     ~~they're~~*

* In Spanish the charachter "h" is pronounced: &lt;á: chě&gt;.

### 3. (Scratched Sapphics)

My magandang ~~Mercia~~ naman.* Don't have any
words for making this better. Sadness,
perfect leavening, tugs the heart's ill-fitting
AIR — ~~hole~~ by its edges.

What capacity feels like: emptiness and
ache. A backwardly line, the needle luring
thread though the holes that've been pierced already. Stars, so
gravity-cooked, they

bead to cushioning blackness. Tell ~~????~~ as much as
need be: ~~I love you.~~ Nothing can worsen how she feels now.
Tell yourself, about anything you need to.
Heart, rest a little.

---

* In Tagalog, "overly beautiful M."

# LAS MENINAS / THE MAIDS OF HONOR

—*Museo del Prado, España*

Thirteen, I stumble
into the princess' gaze.
She's composed, defiant.
Morning slants through
the workshop window
and charges the threads
of her blonde hair.
The Infanta Margarita
wearing a corset so tight
light spikes from it, like
a chest plate worn by
conquistadors in paintings
of Cortés announcing
himself to the Aztecs.

From one maid's tray
la infanta grabs a piece
of amber-colored fruit
that glows warm as a heart,
while the maids search
the porcelain of her face.
Dwarves Maribarbola
and Nicolasito, and a dog,
accompany her, serving
as amusement while
she poses.

Another maid teeters
behind the Infanta, unrumpling
the lace of the princess' sleeve
that goes astray each time
her arm grazes the boughs
of her skirt, boughs wired to
spread the fabric at her waist
and send it tumbling, a tissuey,
stuffed tun to the floor.

The Infanta shows
no regard for Velázquez
who also gazes from inside
the painting, onto the world
that lay beyond the borders
of the painting's framework.
Somehow, Velázquez has
captured that world, too.
The King and Queen of Spain
pose, there. Mere reflections,
they appear as brief, bluish
swaths of paint, in a mirror
that hangs in the background
on a dark rear wall.

All of us onlookers
in the museum's corridor,
standing beside the King and Queen,
a troupe of royal attendees
blued into existence by Velázquez,

who's turned his giant canvas
to obscure our view on
the action of his brush.

How he heaves ochre-sopped
bristles across the oily likenesses,
giving the royals' yards of skin
a taintedness—the illusion that,
with every breath, they ingest
the same bleak air we do,
the room tinged with flecks
of green and purple debris.

I gaze and the Princess
gazes back through me.
She's luminous, a godly idea
etched into human form.
The rest of us abide with her
perfection, infallibility. So much
like the maids who ratchet up
their heavy velvet dresses
that razor dust off the floor.
Those dresses they must harness,
to concoct each step anew
as they try to walk.

# BECOMING

The form letter reads: *If you dream*
*of being Miss USA, this is your chance*
*to turn that dream into reality!*
In disbelief, I turn the envelope over.
*State Pageant Office. Naca*—that's me.
Mail in bio and recent photograph.

Always Miss Nothing in photographs,
I had the desire to fulfill Mom's dream,
Filipina beauty queen, but a fat chance.
By ten, I was shouldering the reality
of a size eighteen blazer. *Not over-*
*weight*, just big, a saleslady braced me,

sensing Mom was about to scold me
from the Casual Corner. That photograph,
lost to the panels of a drawer, I dream
out of me. But this letter reads *chance*—
a word more potent than reality.
At least to a poet mulling over

chance into change, small changings over,
how day-to-day I chance to change me
more permanently. The old photograph,
that suited me, I alter in my dreams.
Thinking it, I set my heart to chance.
Writing it, reality.

So, why not this other reality?—
where my real, my realm is turned over,
exposing some dolled-up, plastic me,
the makings of a bad photograph;
nightmares scare up new dreams to dream.
Why deny myself the chance,

when life's so chancy, chancy
and (perhaps) even destined? Reality
is just most people can't get over
beauty, can't get by or past it. Not me,
my poems, at least, aren't photographic,
symbols perfectly minted from dreams.

They're just a way to outlast reality,
to take my chances and live life over,
and be me, beyond a photograph.

# FALLING, *CALLE ORIZABA*

*—Mexico City*

**1.**

Before I look, I test *aceras* with a rubber foot.          *sidewalks*

A glass leg extends from the street and comes to a hook my hand handles.

Me: a doorstop guffaws over planks of hardwood.

Each step, the arms of a clock tilt closer and closer towards noon.

**2.**

Once I shook my foot loose from a *hueco* in the *asfalto*.         *pothole*

Once I shook my foot and it twinkled like a burned-out fuse.

Once I shook my breath loose inside my lungs and heard the ball-
    bearing's timbal.

Once I shook on a curb, in darkness.

**3.**

Then the filaments of the woozy harp tolled the doorbell.

Then, she held the stringy cheeks of my purpling palms.

I dialed up my feelings: my fingers wound numbers around the rotary
phone's spindle.

Okay. This is me now: her hip bumps the table and the red in the wine-
glass bumbles.

In the bath, my belly button breathes when it comes to the surface.

A knock in the soapy water is just a heartbeat calling.

# WHAT I DON'T TELL MY CHILDREN ABOUT THE PHILIPPINES

*—Lingayen Beach, 1977*

I don't tell lies. Memory's more
beautiful than truth. So I say,
the air was blossoming jasmine trees
and smoke. And it's true.
Clothes boiled in tin tubs. A child,
I watched my uncle splinter
arms of bamboo, his dark skin a blur
in steamy drizzle. A woman
with the burning end of a cigarette
turned inside her lips. Her smile,
a mouth of pink gums squeezed
together. Mornings, my brother and I
raced down the soft belly of the beach,
climbed palm trees—grasping circular rungs
like a throat—to see coconuts churning
in the surf; the skeleton of a torn-down
fighter plane, its snapped propellers,
dented cockpit; fire holes on the beach
where my family came down at night
Dad drank San Miguels and never quit
talking. Filipinos laughed at him.
Mom sat, embarrassed, in the sand.
My cousins, brother, and I stripped cane.
The story ends there for children,

but you wait in bed to hear the rest—
how the air was steam, mosquito incense.
Auntie Marietta set the table. Lanterns
turned her skin red/blue.
I sat in the clubhouse watching
old men play pool till one said
I look old enough to kiss.

## GLOVE

*[She] knocks, saying 'Open for me, my [sister], my love, my dove, my
perfect one' . . . My love thrust [her] hand through the opening, and my
feelings were stirred for [her].*
—Song of Solomon 5: 2-4, from Christiansex.com/fist

She pinches at
the rough seams
where the glove
brows into fingertips
and as she
tugs each digit
the leather tube
suctions flat and
the bottom of
the glove cinches
a cuff around
her thumb-bone
where it angles
into her wrist.
So, the glove,
now, looks like
skin unraveled from
the spokes of
her fingers, or
a bat's wing
as it catches

wind and launches
from the bone's
knuckly masthead. Then,
freeing the butt
of her palm
from the glove,
she flexes her
hand's muscly cheeks
together, skin compressed
so—folded, gullying—
love lines root
in her palm
(the likes only
her lover knew
from slipping on
the bike gloves
she keeps hidden
in the bureau's
top drawer, leather
wilted and milky
from their smallish
hands over-fingering
the throttle's stiff,
rubber grip). With
her fingers relaxed
she withdraws her
dewy hand from
the glove's untapered
back end, spray
of polyester hairs

and must filling
the space between
her face and
her slick skin.
Then, she sets
the gloves down
open ends against
the table where
they stand-up,
each empty nook
having trapped just
enough air for
the bulbs of
skin to appear
natural and improbable
as found sculpture.
How much like
a pianist's utensils
the hands trained
to relax into
near perfect cradles
when she wants
to believe that
the leather's briefed
by her unmannered
or, somehow, unrehearsed
touching. Still warm,
the gloves pose
like their very
own living tissues

keep them up,
the molded leather
surrendering the rest
of her hands'
heat until gloves
gone perfectly cool
harden in place.

# REVENANT GLADNESS

*—for Karina*

The world has sallied forth. Unmeasured, fumigated with acumen,
swearing I heard it. I heard it as *branch* hears its own knobs bear wind,
  and with it . . .
And I saw your eyes climb. Them and your own limbs needle spaces
laid bare in trees' winter's leaf drift, into their passages, little bony cups
the canaling of your ears produce their own echo, What was, is, will be
Worn against the newest weather? In the newest city you return to?
Its eloquence forced upon us the way the air frequents the prongs of
a feather, to underscore as frugal, unspeakable knowledge—how I ask
  (hardly knowing you),
Darling, when you name an unbearable truth, what do you find yourself
  undernaming?
A shiver of false fire, the livery of a place setting beside bowls
of swollen porcelain, justness, air inside our lungs
warmed us stupidly, and the needles lay about bored by hearts gauged to
get stuck against each other needlelessly. *Ay que naca*,
you say when I ask you, What is the translation for "*sin* needles"
  (*adverbio*)?
On the floor and on the pillows, your name was like something laid
  before a doorway a prelude to travel, rose petals, nickels, grains
  of rice
that bloat swallows' bellies—too full and too, overflowingly
There also against diminishment. These days diminishment and
  appearance
aren't opposites—I remind —as much as they are opponents (distant,
  enemy cousins arriving at bookends of a family barbecue).

And I said it to tear the firmament freshly, like stars plucked from
    constellations
to bring her eyes' confusion over forgetting; your top lip against your
    bottom
one in opposing operations. No, not absolutely unlike when words
turn against their truths. The phases of the moon molt the shells off
the crab's back, wax and wane him till he's limp-spined, his all-jelly
    insides
like traitors. Gaze and know my face before waking ruins the fog of my
    actual dream-dusted face!
Come back to the sunshine now rambling
Over the occasion like a mute apology for coming home exactly as I'd
    promised,
gripping green-shooted, leafyparts of beets I'd promised, purple
    knotted artery
talking from my fists. You're on my lap, pounding my chest,
asking for forgiveness for accepting the part of lover who wants me, her,
    her love
to keep coming back in the first place.
We are near each other is what we say, and what you know I promise
    to feel
In the gathered promise of a girl who swirls her coffee before she drinks it,
who dives into a pool eyes open, first,
Who remembers the city as a transparent bride,
Her long hand reaching out of danger to find refuge in your bridle of
    echoey, black hair.

## CORAZÓN COMO UN RELOJ

Los surcos en el sofá azul hacen *tic tac* al tiempo de las reverberaciones de sus caderas.

Los puntos en el techo de yeso esperan, pacientes como trampas para osos.

En la sala, el calor se hace penachos desde las costillas del radiador.

Afuera, ella se escucha mientras que se viene. Los granos brilliantes de arena, paso a paso, se suben por a sus pies.

Cuando ella está relajada, el techo hace *clic*. Cada minuto, se sueltan los muelles.

Revuelve su cara de la cuchara por su taza de café, y el poste se calienta, luego le calienta la mano.

Bajo los colmillos del techo. Bajo el tejado. Bajo las techumbres arcillosas que la abruman, ladrillos rojos y pesados.

La cuchara timbra en la porcelana como timbra el calor en los nudillos del radiador.

Intenta apagarlo, pero no se mueve el mecanismo. La juntura brilla con una patina azul de musgo.

Afuera, una estrella fugaz graba surcos azules por el canto del cielo.

Las válvulas resuenan con el tintinear de los gases calurosos por los
escapes.

Una vez, esperó a unas caderas para calentar los cojines a su lado. Ahora,
ella arde. Ahora, se hincha.

En la cara del reloj, una mano da vueltas mientras—como si bebiera
lengüetadas—la otra mano tiembla inmóvil.

Una pastilla fría y blanca para cuando se hincha el corazón.

Bajo el cielo azul azul. Bajo el vapor que se sube a las nubes, y se derrama
que moja el paisaje como un suave detergente. Bajo el frío cielo
diluido bajo las estrellas. Bajo el camino vago del satélite que
desholleja fotos de la luz, se rompe la distancia como un trozo
de piel.

# HEART LIKE A CLOCK

The groove in the blue couch ticks with the reverberations of her hips.

The points in the ceiling plaster wait, patient as bear traps.

Outside, she can hear herself coming. The glassy kernels of sand, each step, grovel up her foot.

In the living room, heat plumes from the radiator's brass ribs.

While she lies there, the ceiling clicks off the minutes, loosening its springs.

She turns the spoon-face through the coffee, and the metal post heats through, heating her hand.

Beneath the ceiling fangs. Beneath the roof. Beneath the clay shingles bearing down, red and heavy as bricks.

The spoon rings the porcelain like heat ringing the radiator's gut.

She tries to turn it off, but the knob won't budge, the joint sparkled with a mossy-blue patina.

Outside, a shooting star etches a blue groove into the tune of the sky.

The gasses through the heating valves clanging through the traps.

Once, she waited for a set of hips to heat the cushions, next to hers. Now, she smolders there. Now, swells.

On the clock-face, one hand laps around the dial while the other quivers still.

A cool, white pill on the counter for when her heart bells.

Beneath the blue blue sky. Beneath the vapor hoisting itself up into clouds, and spilling over, dousing the landscape like a smoothing detergent. Beneath the cool, diluted heavens beneath the stars. Beneath the random course of a satellite eeking photos out of light, shearing the distance that's a patch of skin.

# REAR WINDOW

We talk on the phone.
My foot in a cast in Heather Green's window.
A single mole climbs the eye of the big toenail.
A toenail that is porous and slick as cornea.
At night while I sleep, the mole slowly creeps
away from me, from the big toe's lunula.
This morning, the sky is wide and translucent.
It is as blue as porcelain as a bathroom sink.
We talk on the phone. Heather Green has packed her things,
dragged them to Adam's and left me this window.
Heather Green: her name is a cortex of modification,
a plural green followed by a veritable one.
When she leaves, I miss her intensity.
So, I sit with my foot in a cast in her window and smoke.
The window is a movie screen I compose before me.
In the proximal foreground, yes, the windowsill, the smoke.
Toes poke out of a cast set on the sill tipsy as a gift-shop Devil's Ivy.
Behind the cast sits two trees, a street, parked cars,
a grade-school building made of brick and windowpanes.
One of the trees accumulates leaves
while the other loses them to an April frost.
We talk on the phone.
In an instant, the leaves have grown old
and their leaf veins pierce their own fragile skin,
tips of those veins now shriveled and thorny.
As he fades the old man watches his fingernails

grow backwards into his hands.

When he scratches he closes his eyes.

The horror of his horns topples the buck.

A bird bathes in dust to wash off the bugs.

We talk on the phone.

The green leaves against the sky were liquid yesterday.

I said, Yesterday, they were a suspension but still liquid, staving off grief.

Today, the curds pulled back from the whey.

We talk on the phone and just like the film,

the leaves die right before my very own eyes.

A blonde is sent to investigate.

My toes curl when the Plains wind casts dust

through the rungs of the empty tree.

Wind, the likely murderess, her blue glances distressing every branch.

Whenever we talk I remember you sat in Heather Green's window

the days before I could stagger from bed.

I went to crutches, one leg, and stuttered before you.

The hammer of a metronome shuddering at one end.

Nights, you cast my leg in plastic bags and used a bowl to bathe me.

I watched light peel from the porcelain.

Dust spangled my reflection you bent with a fist

you made wringing the soap from the foamy washcloth.

Before there was a need for me to talk, for me to even ask,

there was the smoking afterwards of your hands.

There was a wind, there was dust,

and there was the window you had already shut.

There was sweat you drowned in the milky tub.

There was hunger, eggshells hulled-out on the sill.

I ate when you said I was hungry.

I drank because you held a glass up to my lips.

I slept because you lay down beside me.

I dreamt because you were gorgeous and I was dreamy, you said.

I cried because there was ache, and because of you

on the phone there is so much more of the gorgeous ache.

In the mornings, you dressed and redressed, knotting

the silky curtains in the windows when you finished.

When we kissed, brick-ends of the tenement started to echo.

O, we talk on the phone!

Outside a chainsaw's teeth devour the skin

of the faded tree, the wheels of its gut, rings of moonlight.

The reappearance of Heather Green is imminent.

On the phone, she talks about orange-blossom-flavored

tarts she leaves cooling in Adam's window.

From yolk an iodine-soaked appendage is scheduled

to be birthed from the silky insides of my cast.

Quiet as an egg we end without talking.

A new leg to grow back where the cast finally quits

and our good friends, the toes, cork off the ends.

I remember well the well where I drew water.
—*Loretta Lynn*

# HOUSE

**1.**

Everybody lives in a house. The same house but with different trees. Each house finishes at the roof, with a chimney, and antenna for feeding pictures into the TV. Inside is a living room with a wooden floor, or maybe some carpet. And outside, grass sits in the yard thick as carpet. Every house has two or more beds, depending on how many children, or how many relatives live there, how big the beds are. There's also a kitchen, a bathroom, and a place beside the grass to park the car.

A house has houses all around it. You can drive on a street between the houses until you reach the highway, or into the next town Arlington, Virginia, where houses are dotted between Miller's Music Spot and Whitey's Broasted Chicken Restaurant. In Arlington people sit on their steps outside of their houses, or on folding chairs along their small grassy carpets. And I say, "Look at the people in those houses," and my father says, "Those aren't houses, Sweetie. They're shacks."

## 2.

House is a five-letter word. It is pronounced /aus/, /aüs/, or /aüz/.

Looking at these phonetic spellings, you'd probably say, *But wait! What have you done with my 'h'? Where has that chimneystack, cleft of a letter gone to?*

And, *Nowhere*, I say. *Nowhere*, trying to comfort you. *'h' is breathed, not said. A change of direction. A thread of air pulled up your windpipe, expulsion from the gut and lungs. Oh! Oh 'h'! I say, you make health out of wealth, house of a louse, a home of Rome—just conceiving it. The heart and the earth—by the way the wind blows.*

## 3.

I say the word *house* and a beautiful image stirs in your head. Like this, *House*. And then *poof*! The beautiful image stirring in your head. Yes, how beautiful it is with its chimney and windows and front door lowing. How wonderful to house such a beautiful house in your head. How wonderful and immaterial to be a sketch in a bubble that flutters inside you!

## 4.

Once the word house sentenced, "There was a brick house on Macon Avenue." And whenever those words sentenced together, sounds soaked like a bruise, black and blue between them. And though sounds dousing one another wasn't anything new, nor injured no word in particular, still words—as they were known to do—blamed this word and that for their ruin.

Avenue: "Macon, your 'n' is leaving ink clouds, my 'A' dyed blue."
Macon: "Get over it, Avenue. Even capitalized you're common."

The two words nubbed on, 'n' bleeding across the dignified Avenue, while house stood silent—never mind brick leeching the space between them with color. When one day, Macon pitted them against each other.

Macon: "House, have you noticed your stomach growing wider? The round sounds of house filling the mouth whenever you two are mentioned together."

And house was confused. Or just uncommonly distraught when she faced up to brick to ask her:

House: "Brick. Do you notice I'm hardly myself? Just a mass of round sounds. An 'ouse when I sit to one side of you."

Brick: "House, don't blow your stack. Your head's in the clouds again."

House, yet more confused and not as well-mannered as everyone thinks—she's often mistaken for home, her cousin, known as a charming host who throws great parties—chewed out words she'd later regret.

House: "*Brick house*, they say about us. *Brick house*. My 'h' always trampled by the static 'k' makes grinding from the mouth."

But brash 'k' shot up before 'bri-' could stop her.

'k': "Look here, /-k'ouse/. Your 'h' is a foolish place-holder. For 'k' was all friction, and knew not of the ebbs in clausal frailty.

'k': "You know, house, this sentence can sentence without you." As the other sounds begged 'k' not to, she finished it.

'k': "There was a brick on Macon Avenue."

»«

So house was gone, a drifter blowing sentence-to-sentence, 'k'-job to 'k'-job—her specialization. From "a trick house for catching mice and small pests," to the first drafts of "Bleak House" before the typesetting, to odd jobs at "the smoke house," "the break house," "the steak house one must never return to . . . "

Then house, broken, wandered to other sentence, sound-combinations. "We should go to your house," depressed 'h' to a gurgle, next to the rasping and passive-aggressive 'r,' who claimed her pal 's,' "Does the work of you, house, and still more." In "The green house on the left," green was full of advice at the bar.

Green: "You know house, don't complain about 'n.' You need thicker skin. Take 'g,' for example. A green girl—she wouldn't complain."

Then a series of 'b'-jobs, and 'p'-jobs, and 's'-work that bowled the 'h' over. While house slept quietly, 'z' rang in her head.

And for the rest of her days misfortune followed her, sentence, language, country, continent. When house traipsed Europe: *Liaison, liaison, mon amis*, the French words said. In Spanish, 'h' suffered mistaken identity. *¿'Hache' o 'ge' o 'equis' o 'jota,' ¿cuál es su nombre, 'h'?* The Spanish words said.

»«

So house found a quiet spot in the country, just to the right of the silent period. House. And spent her days sounding her name to herself. And wondering if she'd ever be heard from again, started her autobiography.

"Once, there was a house with no 'h.'"

## 5.

Suppose there is a bubble that flutters inside you. Or suppose it builds in the plastic air. Or the plastic that is liquid and luminous yet air. Or suppose in reverse the air plastic. And in its sloshing to-and-fro forms teacups of air unsettling its layers. In the teacups is air air not plastic. And teacups are cool and porcelain as anything that's cool and porcelain. And suppose bubble—though never a bubble before—porcelain and cool as anything once thrown from a wheel, a fired thing, a red thing before it sits and cools on a rack thing, formed of the sloshing that makes bubbles in the plastic air. And bubble air inside of it, an echo of liquid spun into its well. And the echo of heat as liquid brews in the smile that's the bottom of the well.

**6.**

Houses come in two sizes—big and bigger. Since the rich always get richer, there will always be a need for bigger, more gigantic houses. Houses big enough for all the dough they make.

It is not empirically possible to prove the existence of the rich. (So say studies funded by the rich.) Nor possible to prove the existence of the poor. (Cite similar studies.)

## 7.

There are purple houses in America that make a stink with their neighborhood associations. There are enormous red houses we call 'barns' that
stand in the country, where farmers stack their feed, and tools, and sometimes chickens—but for nostalgia—no one mentions them. There are
houses in the warmer states put together of hay bails and dirt and cement-
like fixatives and painted the color of the land and no one, not even the
shifty fox, complains. There are houses made of wood or painted to
resemble wood in the deep forests. And just last summer when neighbors
painted their house 'Cape Cod Grey,' and the rest of us snickered, *But this
is not Cape Cod*, and beside the too-doo a gaggle of book-worms made over
the spelling of *Grey* on a paint can, not-one, single, solitary complaint.
But in America when there is a purple house, it is sure to make a stink
with the neighborhood association. And as sure as it will be a stink, it will
also surely become news in the town newspaper whose name has wedded
and is wistful for the once, great rivalry of Sun, Star, Gazette, and Intel-
ligencers hurrying to report of the comings and goings of the town. And
the paper will re-conceptualize the engagement for a wider audience,
naming it, 'a nasty skirmish,' and then angle it, 'stubborn, purple home-
owner' vs. 'determined, neighborhood association.' And the local-color
piece will play in the Metro section of the Sunday paper people reach for
as if reaching for their toast. And still then, it will not be mentioned how
street lamps gauze the town over in purple, when the cool, dimming light
of August approaches—houses, and sidewalks, the laundry mat windows,
and laundry chiming in the windows of the washing machines, and suds
purpling. And no one hurries to write this, nor bangs door to door for
someone else to witness the phenomena. Nor mentions, however, still,
in the dimming light of August, purple cascades even from pens; so
somehow—even without volition—purple poems are written, telling of
the world awash in plush, August light. And of the purple music box. And

stars through the lens of the periscope. And lovers soothing against each other in the purple heat of August, leaving swatches of color on the sheets beneath them. And that, this purple light is a healing force that showers the tired townspeople, the homeowners, and all of the members of the neighborhood association, the farmers and contractors, hay-bailers and seed-handlers, newspaper reporters, and copy editors, managing editors, and publishers, layout operators, and laundry machinists, poets, and all of the readers who live in the town inside of that poem.

No quiero ya no quiero
la sucia sucia sucia luz del día.
lejana infancia paraíso cielo
oh seguro seguro paraíso.

I don't want anymore don't want
the dirty foul rancid light of day
distance infancy paradise heaven
oh safe certain paradise.

—*Idea Vilariño*

# MANEJAR, I-80 NEBRASKA

Con latigo de madera, un joven sin camisa

rechazaba los penachos de pasto de la pradera.

Detras de él un tren cruzaba pararelo sobre la tierra llanera.

El vidrio tranquilizaba todas las heridas altas.

Bajé las ventanas y las brisas se pincharon

a las briznas filosas de nuestro aliento usado

que se habían desenrollado en la cabina del camión.

No tener prisa para contarlo mientras manejaba ella.

Abandonado, el joven volvía al germen en el retrovisor.

Las pistas se caían a plomo hacia un barranco

que se ha secado y el tren seguía hacia el fondo.

Quizá la palabra sentida sería abismo.

## DRIVING, I-80 NEBRASKA

A boy bare-chested with a switch

beat back the plumes of the prairie grasses.

Behind him a train filed parallel over the plain land.

The glass tranquilized any loud wounds.

I rolled down the window and breezes

needled the wooly ends of used-up breath

that had unspooled into the truck cabin.

No hurry to tell the story as she drove.

The boy went to seed in the rearview mirror.

The tracks plummeted into a defunct ravine

and the train followed down the hollow.

Or, was the right word for it chasm.

# WITNESS

My cousin Sonny missions with her kids in the Philippines.

In Pittsburgh, Constance and Reyanne come to the door. We've met
before at another address.

Through the lead-glass window: they straighten their scarves, teeth,
when they hear footsteps clanging near the door.

They don't remember my stream-lined teeth, my globy lips or eyes from
all the heads they meet.

*My cousin Sonny's a Witness, too*, I tell them. *She missions with her kids in
the Philippines.*

Down Atlantic Avenue, a year before, I said, *Come back and meet Faith, the
owner. She's new in town and needs to make more friends.*

Today, they ask if I follow faith and I decline, *an atheist.* And they ring
their knuckles—screw fingers around their moldy joints like a nut-
cracker's teeth.

*My cousin Jing Jing—Sonny's sister—a Witness, too*, I say as they clang the
pages of their good books, fingering for a tooth of conversation.

Constance and Reyanne don't rush into talking. Mornings, they buzz by
the doors like flies.

And I'm patient with them—out of respect for the cousins—while teeming in the hot, Pittsburgh dust I carry in a suitcase from home to
home.

*Jing Jing is my favorite name,* is what I long to tell them. *What's your favorite
name?* I long to ask.

Once, in Seattle, I was bald and breezes slid easily from my gut. I'd say,
*Make like the Jehovah's Witnesses and count me out.*

Once, Sonny and Jing came out to the S.F. Airport to see Puring and me
as we stretched our good leg out to the Philippines.

They kept a glowy silence about my head as we teetered past the clanging
Krishnas.

Love balled through my bare skin. A brilliant passport.

In the P.I., Puring and I visited Uncle Ulpiano—their father—a stroke
had left a golden sore in his eye.

Faith is a photo of Ulpe, a Ranger in WWII, closed in the dusty pages of a
book, his corners shrunken and torn, footless from all the marching.

A friend of my grandfather's taught Ulpe to read. For the god's-sake of
this story, we'll call her Faith.

Constance and Reyanne smile when I say: *"I bequeath myself to the dirt
to grow from the grass I love"*; then they frown, "Our souls just mush
under *bootsoles,* long to be eaten by grassy teeth."

Ulpe doesn't recognize my brilliant head. Thinks I'm the younger
brother. My name nonsense.

With the Pacific conquered, Truman took the ones who read and sent
the rest packing.

When Constance and Reyanne hit the books again, I want to say, faith
and belief, a foggy bathroom mirror, a raincoat on the man who
drags a suitcase full of dictionaries door to door.

Today's forecast, humidity: I heat myself, I heat my hand, I heat the air
inside my hand like a handful of warm, glass marbles.

I can't believe they call me Sister anyway. When they're just Constance
and Reyanne to me, the same as Jing and Sonny.

Their pamphlet charges to my sweat and releases a green sore of ink in
my palm.

# THE ADORATION AT EL MONTAN MOTOR LODGE

*—San Antonio, TX. Reviews not yet available.*

A leathery tobacco stain where her knuckle creases.

*Limón* in the taco grease licked off of lovers' fingers.

Tonight the sheets will yellow beneath the dim light bulbs.

A yellow kiss. *love plagues the Earth*.

How water from the marred glass roughens her top lip.

Exhaust the nylon rug kicks up. The pink sink. The mirror above the sink that forces a ripple through her gut. The smile that's a water-stain on the smoky curtains. A pillow that—for the most part—lovers use for balancing. The cataract bluing the tube inside the ancient TV set. The showers that run all day and swell the hallway with their sweat. The dewy pillow against her face. A plague of love upon her.

For hours the lovers' feet kick at the woozy nightstand.

*Santa Biblia* in gold leaf on the good book on the nightstand.

Brown nipples that start to fade as she ages, that metallic pussy smell, how the grain of her cunt toughens around her fingers when she comes, the veneer of as a mouth.

Blood that starts to slough off once her breath has dried it to her lips.

Combing fingers through the red carpet fronds, searching for her glasses.

Side-by-side the blisters raise in the shape of teeth.

## WHILE WATCHING *DALLAS*, MY FILIPINA AUNTIE GROOMS ME FOR WORK AT THE MASSAGE PARLOR

Friday nights, the images
of hot tubs, Manhattans,
and blondes fingering the hair
on Cliff Barnes' chest tickled
my Auntie Linda until she cried,
*Aiiieeeee!* Auntie Ning beside her
rolled cotton balls in tubes
she used to dab the cheap nail
polish that pooled between
her cuticle and skin.

Days, Auntie Linda worked
at Hair Cuttery. In her chair,
clients were mortified to hear,
*Sagging breasts means sagging hair,*
as Linda parted their wet mops
down the middle for effect.
Nights, I painted my nails
*Pearlucious.* I begged for *Ruby Red.*
But Linda said, *That's an old,*
*white ladies color. They leave quarters.*
*Their husbands leave watches.*

Auntie Ning hiked up a pant leg,
and I dug my fingers into her calf.

She writhed and slapped at the thin rug,
tossed over holes in the thinning carpet.
Meanwhile, J.R. tippled scotch.
Close-up, wordlessly, he scolded me
for carving grids in the lotion
I lathered on Ining's legs.
Ice clinked in J.R.'s glass. Crystal,
it twinkled in the light. He took
a swig and said, *If you point*
*a double barrel shot gun at me,*
*you better fire both barrels.*

Linda worked on Ning with
a chopping motion that prompted
her to tell the story of how she
wanted to karate chop the neck
of gentlemen clients who waited
by her car to ask her out. I was ten.
Even then, I figured she also
meant my father, who teased her
at dinner, *You touch dirty old men,*
when every morning he tramped
the hallway in a towel, his package
swashbuckling hip to hip.

When I rubbed Linda's tiring
hands, she said I should work
with her, Saturdays nights,
*tips plus ten bucks an hour.*
Sue Ellen carried John Ross to the jet.
Back then I wondered, who calls

a child by such an adult name?
The child who, a season later,
is eight years old. After two more,
he turns fourteen. A hiatus and
he returns to Southfork, to learn
to pick flesh and blood
apart just like his father.

## SEGUIR

Un pescador
en la cama del río,
un gusano
tan enfriado como
leche en la mano,
ensarta el anzuelo
anillo a través
de los bulbos
de la carne.
Penetrado
se afloja
como una cintilla
que se quita
de la rueda
y se llena
con polvo.
El cielo está gris.
El pescador
coge la caña,
trozo de plomo
con forma de lágrima,
lastra
la línea de seda,
a la vez que hunde
su palma
en el corque

del mango.
Al tirar la línea,
dibuja semicírculos
en el aire,
ese movimiento sutil
como una hoz
y el aire suelta
una soporosa queja
mientras la línea
siega por encima.
La línea vacila,
sobre la expansión
de agua, gira
el cilindro de la trampa
de la línea tan rápido
que el huso chirria
como lo misma
pena de las visagras
de la puerta enojada.
El pescador espera
oír el sonido
roto por el projectil
el silencio del agua
antes de buscar
la carnada donde
las pequeñas ondas
se combaten por
el agua más allá.

## *SEGUIR:* TO FOLLOW, KEEP ON, CONTINUE

A fisherman
on a river bed,
a worm
cool as milk
in his hand,
threads his silver
hook through
the bulbs of
the worm's body.
Pierced
it goes slack
as tape drawn off
a wheel and
sated with dust.
The sky is gray.
The fisherman
grabs his pole,
tear-shaped iron
weights ballast
the fishing line
as he sinks
his palm into
the groove he wears
and wears into
the handle's cork.
Casting he loops
the line behind him

and swings it
keen as a sickle
and the air lets go
of a sleepy groan
when the line
mows over it.
The line across
the water's
expanse spins
the barrel of the
fishing line's trap,
so fast the spindle
moans like an angry
door's hinges.
Then the fisherman
waits for a plunk
·before he searches
for his bait
where the ripples
already gang up
in the water
beyond him.

# IN THE TIME OF THE CATERPILLARS

Auntie Ining renders fat from slabs of pork she's cut into cubes.

At the kitchen table, I render "Scene from the Garden of Gethsemane" in chalk, in the backdrop a greasy staccato.

Sweeten your tongue to the roof of your mouth till /e/s come out, if you want to pronounce Auntie I's name.

Today begins Elvis week and I's heart pounds, Elvis sweetening her meaty lining.

Though her name's the shape of an "I," Auntie I's the shape of an O. In childhood fotos an O. A wonder she's ever known love.

A returning G.I., E's sweet on a girl rendered helpless when she loses her top in the staccato of waves.

At the party that night, he renders a song he sweetens with dance, a shag in his tail for the swoony damsels.

When I look down, eyelids of apostles are sweetened shut from too much dust, all my overtouching.

When Elvis clenches his jaw as someone else speaks, it's all his overacting.

Tupelo, Mississippi, 1929. A child who would be a very tan king is born.

On the TV Elvis soothes the savage gypsies who store booty in a shiny
    caboose; the Acapulco cliff divers; shirtless, trapeze artists; a tizzy
    of dizzy love-hung women; seriously, devoutly, desperately nuns;
    bullfighters—make that one. *Ah, but Don Pedro can this one sing?*

All along, the black gum in our front yard fizzes with caterpillars;
    locusts scorch the sky with a sticky, torch song.

In some other cases, the black gum's rendered, the black tupelo and the
    tupelo gum.

In waves the curious neighbors clench at the brown woolies barking up
    the black gum's skin.

"Green surrenders to a staccato of Os," goes the leaves' fading stomata.

When the black gum's leaves go faint and holy, my parents put their feel-
    ers on.

At dusk, the dusty apostles also fade as Christ begs for strength in the
    face of death!

How the silky caterpillars litter the pavement, falling through the holes
    they've eaten, to death.

With our fingers, we clench ice cream scoops between saltines, sweeten
    avocado with sugar and swoon.

When Auntie I rings fizz from the Os of a sponge, her fingers bark from all the bleaching.

"She's as big as a house," Mom and Dad pound her when she isn't around or isn't looking.

She steeps her branch in the murky water, fingers for the rice sweetening the bottom of the pan.

*Pick your poison*, says the neighbor, a peevish red bud blooming in his yard.

Gripped with love, I pound white rice until I'm full, white bread till I'm numb.

A chalk of scorched meat on the bottom of the pan. An oily O on the chicharrón rag.

Outlines of apostles I've fingered into Os, even scalded with grease they keep sleeping.

When Dad starts with war buddies burning monkeys from trees, Mom goes to sweep the brown woolies to the street.

I gum on the chewy chicharrón bark, at the fatty white parts: hard swallow.

If food is love, pound-for-pound, Auntie Ining's *a hunk o' hunk o'*.

*Wise men say:* "When Christ calls, fill his jug with laughter, his eye sockets with song."

No black people sun in *Blue Hawaii*, nor *Fun in Acapulco*, *ni viven en Las Vegas tampoco*, leaving one explanation: too tan.

In a canoe Elvis fingers his tiny instrument. O flaming ukulele of passion! Ukelele of desire!

*What a gas.* Dad pounds his foot, sweetening his story with, *The singed bodies fizzed.*

Elvis, have you ever known love? Have you ever never wanted the girl and still known love?

A ticked off Mom and Dad tweeze bodies with fingers through their spiny hair.

I watch them in wonder through the kitchen window, the two Os in the front of my head.

## HABLAR ESPAÑOL SIGUE ASÍ

Un pájaro en el árbol canta a un papagayo en la jaula, en el piso al lado.

Mientras patina, la aguja toca los surcos labrados en el vinilo del álbum.

Frente a la carnicería un hombre, nombre de una mujer tatuado en el pecho.

Las letras en su pecho se enverdecen con los años.

CHRISTINA. ¿Quién es esta mujer de piel?

En la periferia, las ráfagas verdes escapan los antiguos apilados de humo.

Su olor en la funda de la almohada demora su salida.

Una boca verde, el gusto de los rastros en su lengua y sus labios.

Una pulpa de estrellas por el colador del cielo grueso y negro.

La gente que vive dentro del pueblo dice la nombre, << Lincoln-coma-Nebraska >>.

El pájaro que canta en el árbol se vuela al cantar el papagayo.

En una noche sin estrellas, manejamos sin tracción contra el terreno de cielo liso.

¡O ruedas que giran! Nadie muere del despecho demasiado rápido.

Sólo ecos de sudor y de ella nada.

## SPEAKING SPANISH IS LIKE

A bird in a tree sings to a parrot in a cage, next door.

As the needle skids it plays the grooves carved in the record vinyl.

In front of the butcher shop a man, the name of a woman tattooed on his chest.

The letters on his skin go green from too many years.

*CHRISTINA*. Who is this woman on the skin?

On the edge of town, green gusts escape the aging smoke stacks.

The smell of her in a pillowcase delays her leaving.

A green mouth, the taste of rastro* on her tongue and lips.

A pulp of stars through the sieve of Nebraska's thick, black sky.

People inside this town call it, "Lincoln-comma-Nebraska."

The bird in the tree takes flight when the parrot joins in.

On a night without stars, we drive, no traction to the sky's smooth terrain.

---

\* los rastros: meatpacking plants

O spinning wheels! No one dies from a broken heart too quickly.

Only echoes of sweat and the rest of her gone.

# IN MEXICO CITY

City of misses.

City of echoes.

City of transformer explosions in the distance.

City of long plastic pipe over workmen shoulder blades,

that criss-cross the sky like a skeleton.

City of want to edifice itself. City of look upwards.

City of rivulet. City of rubble. City of particle, granule, and grain.

City of Oriental flower motifs transposed onto huipiles,

that waitresses wear at the Sanborn's café.

City slowly paving the sky with crumb and tinge and trace.

City of permeate. City of discern.


City of ascending concrete columns.

And of the dangling tailpipe. City you wade through curls of exhaust.

Of pilgrims hauled on the flatbed of trucks, weighed down

by guilt and shame and forgive and humble and mercy and apology.

City of concrete-colored air and concrete-colored breath,

where cheap tires leave tar varnish on the street,

of concrete hearts—yours so solidly not in-love with me.


City of faces on a metro.

City of smog. City of frown and accelerated aging.

City of train tires whistling over train tracks.

City where your silence is roomy as a train car.

City of muffle, of transfer, of big readers, of stare.

City where I'm too tall to be Mexican, I'm too red to be Indian.

Where my traits escape powers of discernment.

City of wrestle past bodies pressed close as you exit.

City of excuse me, of permit me, of pardon.

City of the averted gaze, where with a direct gaze you say, *I want you.*


City of no water, no light, no gas.

City of furnaces and lost eyelashes.

City so high up even passion lacks heat.

Where breath lacks earthen, human smell, the smell of shedding.

City of perpetually watched pots and instant coffee.

City where I should have asked for love like rent, up front.


City where water crowns from stolen faucet heads.

Of unmelted sugar at the bottom of glasses.

Where lukewarm juice drowns complaints at the *lunchería.*

Where bartenders inquire on the roots of your tongue.

*Repeat after me, 'Pulque, pulga, pulmón,'* he says.

City of spirits fermented with spit, where you *Just swallow. Don't taste it.*


City of gas bells, church bells, trash bells, *sandía,* and *camote.*

City where a Rottweiler barks on a rooftop and mariachis trumpet in the
plaza.

City of the silicon earplugs.

Of club girls and DJs leaving for Germany.

Of Yaneth's mad crushes on Germans.

Of blow and overflowing sinks.

City of laptops adrift on flooded tile floors.

City of wee, and toilets you flush with a bucket of water. City of stool.

City of ashy doorbells and pushpins,
of anonymous dress form mannequins,
of dropping keys to a lover from a fourth-floor window,
of key teeth and finicky key holes.
City of the immaculate alignment.
City where I called your name like something from Calvino,
*Karina! Karina!* I shouted at your window.
City of txt msgs, *Sore but I miss you.*
*Pendejada pero fabulosa, amorcita güerita chingona...*

City of basilicas and pilgrims and skinned knees.
Where a morenita watched you crawl to the Virgen.
City of candles beginning to spit at the over-crowded alter of San Diego.
Every prayer he's answered.
City of *centavos* and *sueltos* on street corners,
of *horoscopos* printed on wooden-match boxes.
City where I pinch off the flame after licking my fingers.

City where underground cities upturn cobblestones,
that unearthed are displayed in the Zócalo.
City where they piled earthquake victims in the stadium.
City of remember, of rumble, of growl.
City where I fell in a hole and I wanted to die.
City where I sat on the curb and cried.
City where my foot sagged like a snapped tree limb.
City where I was stuck full of pushpins.
City where I howled into a pillow when I got back to bed.
City where I held it in and sweat.

· · ·

City where you sat at the foot my bed to bear witness.

Where I bawled before you, and felt that moment the deepest sense of
witness.

As you watched speechlessly and did not judge.

Where you returned to the accident scene and found a girl's shoe.

Where there's a hole as long as I kept longing for you.


City where all Sandra's warnings pretty much came true: city of hazard,
city of spill, city of hustle, city of tweak, city of the too frequently
mopped floor.

*In Mexico City, you learn to walk with an eye-patch or cane.*

City where I limped through a crowd of the lame, down a street of
*farmácias.*

City where I practiced my tenses: have limped, had limped, had been
limping.

City where I limped (meaning yesterday).

City where I limped (meaning my entire life).

City where I tensed before taking a step.

City where change is better kept in your pocket.

And where every outstretched palm is a prayer.


»«


Oh, palm tree with the disheveled, turned out folds of bark.

Pummelled, volcano rock used for decorative edging in Cuauhtémoc
Park.

Filets of orange meat pierced through and stood up on a spit, cork-
shaped, shaved and cooked until the shards heap up on a foamy grill.


· · ·

Sometimes love looks worse than it is,
the ring of grit at the hem of a pant leg,
the black on the bottom of a kettle.

# CATCHING CARDINALS

*—Annandale, Virginia*

For a week, he stacked dusty sacks
of birdseed in a kitchen corner,
and we acted like the towering stack
wouldn't topple us during dinner.

His booby-trap, white cotton twine,
a stick, and a pen he put together
from two by fours and chicken wire
peeled off a thorny ream at Hechinger's.

Out of nowhere, the gold-plated cage—
the same gold cage where, for years,
lived our pet cockatoo, who spent all day
spitting seed husks on the furniture.

Then, one night, Dad cut up bread
with scissors. I woke up with the smells
of coffee, menthol cigarettes, and sweat
burning the skin inside my nostrils.

I dashed to a window to watch him
and my brother. In a shallow slant
in the yard, they hid out, ready to rip
the cord and walk away red bird in hand.

They chased bluejays with rocks. Swarms
descended. I heard the screen door snap.
I still picture streaks of blood down his arms
from wrestling blackbirds from his trap.

It took days for Dad to capture his prize.
Once he did, I remember, I looked
at this wild thing and wondered why
it was so important. How it shrieked, bled,

and shoved its beak through the rods,
into the unbound air.

# NOTES

The song "Gavilán o Paloma," "The Hawk or the Dove," was written and performed by José José.

"Becoming" and "Revenant Gladness" are after Ann Lauterbach poems.